Three Little Funny Ones
Charlotte Hough

Oliver and Timmy and Tom are always up to
something. They are the best of friends and they
have lots of funny adventures – and some scary
ones too, like being mistaken for three mangold
wurzels by an old cow and catching a sausage
dog in their lion trap!
 Five lively stories full of mischief and fun!

Charlotte Hough has written a number of
children's books. She lives in London.

Three Little Funny Ones

Written and illustrated by Charlotte Hough

PUFFIN BOOKS

PUFFIN BOOKS

Published by the Penguin Group
Penguin Books Ltd, 27 Wrights Lane, London W8 5TZ, England
Penguin Books USA Inc., 375 Hudson Street, New York, New York 10014, USA
Penguin Books Australia Ltd, Ringwood, Victoria, Australia
Penguin Books Canada Ltd, 10 Alcorn Avenue, Toronto, Ontario, Canada M4V 3B2
Penguin Books (NZ) Ltd, 182–190 Wairau Road, Auckland 10, New Zealand

Penguin Books Ltd, Registered Offices: Harmondsworth, Middlesex, England

First published by Hamish Hamilton 1962
Published in Puffin Books 1968
This edition published by Viking Kestrel 1987
Published in Puffin Books 1989
10 9 8 7 6 5 4 3

Printed in England by Clays Ltd, St Ives plc

Contents

The Duck-Pond

Once upon a time there were three little houses with three little gardens, all in a row.

Each little house had a little boy living in it. One was called Oliver,

- one was called Timmy,

and one was
called Tom.

Instead of standing on their
feet and talking sensibly, like
most people, they did funny

things, like standing on
their heads

and not talking sensibly at all,
so their mothers called them
the three little funny ones.

Each little boy had something
special. Oliver had a
yellow cart,

Timmy had a little sister,

and Tom had a
trumpet and a big
straw hat.

One day they all went out for
a walk along the road outside
their houses and before long they

met some ducks going for
another walk.

Flip-flop, flip-flop, went the ducks on their flat feet. They were enjoying the sunshine. Flip-flop, flip-flop, but they never looked behind them.

"Look out!" cried Oliver, Timmy and Tom. They could see a naughty little sausage-dog galloping down the road in a cloud of dust. He was coming to chase the ducks.

"Come along!" cried Mrs Duck to her children, all in a hurry, "Come along!"

The poor little ducks couldn't run very fast. They were so much better at swimming. Flipflopflipflop, flipflopflipflop, but it wasn't nearly fast enough.

So Tom jumped out in front of
the naughty sausage-dog and
blew as hard as he could on his
trumpet: Parpity-parp PARP!
went the trumpet. The
sausage-dog nearly fell over
backwards with surprise.
"Grrr-WOW!" he said in a loud
voice. He didn't like other people
making more noise than he
could.

Oliver picked up Mrs Duck
and put her in the yellow cart,

and Timmy picked up the little
ducklings, one, two, three, four,
five, six, and put them in the
straw hat.

Then they all ran as fast as
they could down the road to the
duck-pond. Oliver lifted Mrs
Duck carefully out of the cart
and put her carefully on to the
water and Timmy emptied one,
two, three, four, five little
ducklings out of the hat, but oh
dear, there should have been six.

The three little boys had dreadful thoughts about the sausage-dog. *"What have you done with the last little duckling?"* they asked.

The dog rolled his eyes at them and looked sad and good. "Well . . ." said Oliver doubtfully, "Well . . ." He didn't know if the sausage-dog was a good actor or not.

"That's a funny thing," said
Timmy suddenly to Tom, "listen
to your trumpet!" The trumpet
was lying on the bank where
Tom had dropped it and it was
talking to itself, but instead of
saying "Parp-parp" it was saying
"peep-peep".

They all stared at the trumpet.
"Peep-peep!" it said very crossly,
"Peep-peep!" and out walked the
last little duckling. The sausage-

dog was too astonished to catch
it. Down it went to the edge of
the water and *plop*, all the duck
family were together again in the
pond.

Round and round their mother
swam the little ducklings. The
sausage-dog sat on the bank and
watched. "Gr-ow!" he cried
excitedly, "Grrrrr-ow!" He did
so want to catch the ducks, but
he hated getting
his feet wet.

The
Mouse

The three little funny ones and
Timmy's little sister sat on the
bank and watched the baby ducks

bobbing about like fluffy corks
and saying peep peep.

"When they get bigger they'll
say 'Quack quack'," said Tom.
Timmy's little sister pointed her
finger. She couldn't talk very
much but she could smile. She

could see a little mouse swimming across the pond.

Mice don't swim very fast, so Timmy's little sister ran straight into the pond before Timmy could

stop her and she caught the mouse quite easily. The water came right

up over her white dress, but she
didn't mind.

"Oh, she is naughty!" cried
Timmy. "She never even took
her white shoes and socks off!"
So they all rushed in to fetch her.

But the bottom of the pond was all soft and muddy so they all paddled about a bit. When they came out they all had black legs, and Timmy's little sister was black to her waist.

Timmy looked rather anxious. "Never mind," he said. "Whatever happens, we've got the mouse." But, oh dear what a pity, Timmy's little sister had dropped it. He was ashamed of

her. It was disappointing. They
looked and looked, all round the
duck-pond, but they couldn't find
it anywhere. The mouse had run
into the long grass of the
meadow where he had a little
hole.

"How very black our legs
are!" said Tom, and because
they were such funny ones they
all blacked their faces to match.

Then they stuck some leaves in
their hair and looked at
themselves in the water. They
did look odd.

They made funny faces and
danced round the pond.

The mouse had to fetch his
wife to come and look.

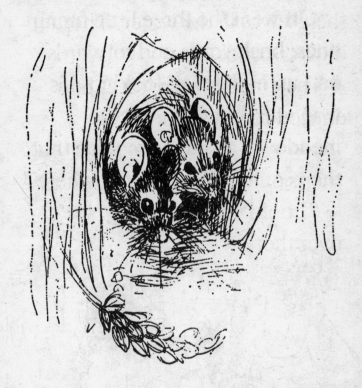

"My goodness!" said Timmy,
stopping all of a sudden and
looking round, "What's
happened to my sister?" She was

so small that she had got quite
lost. It was worrying.

Off went the three little funny
ones, backwards and forwards
and up and down, looking this
way and that way, but the
meadow was such a big one that
they couldn't find her anywhere.

"Look!" cried Oliver, "she's
over there!"

"No," said Timmy, "she's over there!"

But when they looked carefully the wind was waving the tops of the grass all over the meadow.

"We don't know *where* she is!" cried Tom. "It all looks the same!"

Timmy's little sister was sitting
in the long grass picking flowers
and she had very sharp eyes. She
could see the mice. "Aba?" she
said to the mice in her soft little
voice, "Aba?"

"Squeak!" said the mouse's
wife in a friendly way. She
wasn't afraid of a baby.

Timmy's little sister offered the mouse's wife her flowers. The mouse's wife sniffed them. Then she picked one up and pulled it into her house.

Timmy's little sister poked another flower into the hole and watched while it slowly disappeared. Then she did it again. Inside, the mouse's wife was very busy making them all up into her bed. It did smell nice.

Presently all the flowers were gone. Timmy's little sister felt rather naughty. She enjoyed being lost.

The little boys were quite tall. Their round black heads came above the tops of the grass, just like three mangold wurzels growing on three little stalks. Up and down the meadow and backwards and forwards went their three worried faces with the leaves on top.

"Aha!" thought a cow, who was standing in the distance and looking at them thoughtfully. "I'm getting tired of grass. Mangold wurzels would make a nice change for my lunch, and it must be nearly lunchtime now."

She walked slowly towards the three little funny ones. She was rather fat. They looked at her. She was a very big cow. The little boys started to walk home. The cow walked faster. She lowered her head so that she could see them more easily. "A *very* nice change," she said to herself.

The three little funny ones started to run, swish swish through the long grass. It was hard to run through. Oliver

bumped into Timmy and Timmy bumped into Tom. Tom fell down and hurt his knee but he tried not to cry.

When the tears had cleared away Tom saw Timmy's little sister sitting in the buttercups not far off. He pulled at the legs of Oliver and Timmy. "*She* knows how to get away from that old cow," he said. "We shall have to get lost in the grass too."

So they all made themselves as small as they could and crawled off very carefully through the long grass so as not to disturb it too much. They pretended they were worms. It was rather fun.

The cow found that her mangold wurzels had disappeared. "Mooo!" she said in a disappointed voice. "Mooo!"

Never mind, she had seen some thistles. "They aren't quite as *filling* as mangold wurzels, thistles aren't," she said to herself, "but I must say they're really very tasty."

A Trap
for Lions

"Well, I never did!" said the
mothers of Oliver, Timmy and
Tom when they got back home.
"You look exactly like three old
mangold wurzels. Go along at
once and wash your faces."

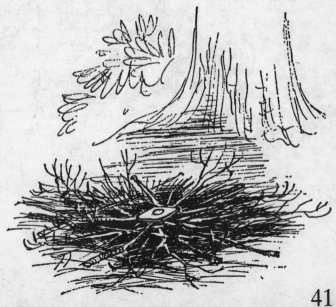

So all the little boys went up to Timmy's bathroom and washed off the mud so that they didn't look like mangold wurzels any more. And because they were such funny ones they had a little splashing game afterwards and some of the water dripped

through the floor on to Timmy's
mother underneath and she
came running upstairs, very
cross.

She made them mop up the
floor.

"You must stay in the garden
this afternoon and not get into

mischief," she said. "But don't
come near the house because
you might make too much noise
and the baby has to have her
rest."

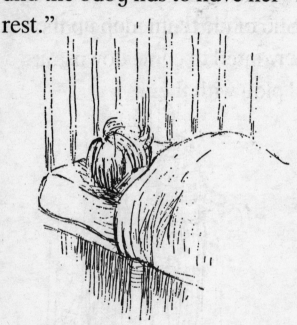

"What shall we do?" said the
three little funny ones to each
other after lunch. Timmy's little
sister was in her cot. They could

hear her singing quietly to
herself in her bedroom.

They sang back. The baby
sang much louder. She stood up
in her cot and rattled the bars.
She wanted to come downstairs
and play with them.

"Go away!" said Timmy's
mother.

The three little funny ones went down to the bottom of the garden. There was a tree and some bushes.

Oliver looked over the fence to the meadow where the duck-

pond was. "It's a pity we haven't got a pond in the *garden*," he said.

Suddenly they all had the same idea. That often happened to the three little funny ones. They decided to dig a pond underneath the tree. They all fetched spades from their tool-sheds and dug for a long time.

Their arms ached. "That's big enough," said Tom, "now we can fill it with water."

They went to Timmy's mother's kitchen and filled the yellow cart and the big straw hat with water. The water dripped

through the hat and it slopped over the side of the cart when they pulled it along and made rather a mess on the floor, but

they ran very quickly down to
the hole they had dug so that
there was still some left to make
the pond.

Then they ran back to the
kitchen for some more water.
The mud on their feet made
marks on the wet floor.

When they got back to the pond they found it was just a dry hole again. All the water had soaked away. It was very disappointing.

"We shall have to be quicker still," said Oliver.

They ran back to the kitchen but there was Timmy's mother, mopping the floor. "Not in here," she said.

"But we're making a pond. We've dug a special hole for it."

"Not a pond," said Timmy's mother. She did look firm.

"What shall we do with the hole then?"

"Why don't you put a plank of wood across it and make it into a car? Then you could go for a ride in it," said Timmy's mother. But they didn't feel like making a car.

"Well, why don't you put a plank of wood across it and make it into a boat? Then you could sail it to Africa and see the lions," said Timmy's mother. But they had made a boat before.

"They wouldn't be *real* lions," said Tom. "I wish we had a *real* lion, just a little one."

"I know!" cried Oliver, "we'll catch a real one in our hole. We'll make it into a trap for lions!"

That *was* a good idea.

"It's only a small trap so it ought to catch a small one," said Tom, who did so want a dear soft little cuddly lion-cub. "We don't want a big one."

Timmy's mother gave them a biscuit to tempt the lion-cub into the hole and they spread some branches over the top so that he wouldn't be able to see the trap until he had trodden on it and fallen in.

"He won't hurt himself, will he?" asked Tom.

Oliver thought that lions were like cats.

"They always fall on their feet," he said.

When the trap was quite finished the three little funny ones climbed up into the tree so that they could watch the lion-cub when he came along and fell into the trap.

It was fun sitting in the tree at first. They could see into each

other's gardens and they could
see Mrs Duck and her babies on
the pond and the cow in the
meadow. Through Timmy's
window they could see his
mother lifting his little sister out
of her cot and putting on her
woolly jersey.

"Is anything coming yet?"
"What a long time he's taking!"
The branches of the tree were

so hard and scratchy. The three
little funny ones decided to hide
in the bushes instead.

"We must sit very still," said
Oliver, "so as not to frighten him
away."

But it was so dark and tickly,
and Oliver, Timmy and Tom
were not very good at sitting still.
They decided that it was time for
tea.

"The lion-cub will come while
we're indoors," said Tom.

"We can just come out and
collect him afterwards," said
Oliver.

It was exciting. All the same,
they were very hungry.

In the middle of tea Tom
looked out of the window and
saw that it had started to rain.
"Oh dear!" he said, "the poor
lion-cub will be getting wet. I'd
better go down and fetch him
now." So he put on his straw hat

and ran down to the bottom of
the garden.

There was a loud rustling and thumping going on in the lion-trap and the branches were moving on the top. Tom pulled his hat down on to his nose, which made him feel braver.

"Of course," he said to himself, "it's not much use coming down here without a piece of string to tie round his neck. I'll have to go back and get some."

So he ran up to his house. "Well," said his mother, "have you caught one?"

"Oh yes," said Tom, "I've come for some string to lead him back with."

"What is he like?" asked his mother.

"I don't know, I couldn't see him."

"Why not?"

"My hat was over my eyes."

"Can I come and see him too?" asked Tom's mother.

Tom took her hand. 'Don't expect a big one,' he said. 'There isn't room for anything bigger than a cub.'

So they fetched the others and they all ran down to the lion-trap. The scuffling was still going on.

"'It's *very* small," said Oliver doubtfully, peering down through the branches.

"It's black," said Timmy.

And what do you think it was? It was that silly old sausage-dog!

Bobo
Angela

The boys made the lion-trap into a little house and sat there making plans. The sausage-dog was with them.

"He's not much of a lion," said Oliver.

"No, but we could make him into a horse," said Tom, taking the piece of string out of his pocket. "I'll make some harness out of this and then he can take Bobo Angela for a ride in the cart."

Bobo Angela was Timmy's little sister's doll. Luckily the sausage-dog already wore a kind of harness so it was quite easy to fix him to the cart. Bobo Angela

just fitted snugly inside and Timmy's little sister jumped about and clapped her hands. She loved playing with the three little funny ones.

The sausage-dog made quite a good horse at first and pulled the yellow cart very nicely. They all walked slowly along the road together until they came to the postman's house. The postman's cat was sitting in the sun outside the front door.

As soon as the sausage-dog reached the postman's house and saw the cat he forgot that he was supposed to be a horse and only remembered that he was a bad old dog that liked chasing things. The cat jumped across the ditch and went through the hedge and into a garden and through a stream and under another hedge, and so did the dog and the cart and Bobo Angela. And so did the three little funny ones but rather far behind because it was so difficult.

When they came out of the other side of the second hedge the sausage-dog was far away in the distance and they couldn't run nearly fast enough to catch up.

They ran through the village
and across the bridge down to
the little wood at the bottom of
the hill. There they found the
yellow cart turned upside down.

Poor Bobo Angela must have
fallen out on the way. They
looked for her all the way home
but they couldn't find her
anywhere.

They did everything they
could to cheer up Timmy's little
sister. They stood on their heads
and walked on their hands and
pulled funny faces and turned
head over heels, but still she went
on crying.

"You'll just have to go and
look for Bobo Angela again,"
said her mother, "and look very,
very carefully this time."

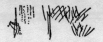

They looked everywhere they
could think of. Timmy's little
sister clung on to his hand and
wailed.

They found the postman's hen
sitting on her eggs under a gorse-
bush. Timmy's little sister

stopped crying and pointed her
finger. "Ook!" she cried, "Ook!"

Timmy arranged the gorse-
bush carefully so that the hen
was hidden. "If nobody finds the
eggs," he told her, "they'll hatch
out into fluffy chickens."

They looked very carefully everywhere and they found quite a lot of other things. They found a button with an anchor on it, a dragonfly, a grass-snake, the footprints of a man with a wooden leg and a lucky horse-shoe, but they never found Bobo Angela.

"We've been everywhere the sausage-dog went about three times over," said Oliver sadly at last. It really began to look as if Bobo Angela must have got up and walked herself away!

The three little funny ones felt so guilty. "Never mind," they said to Timmy's little sister, "we'll all go home and make you a dragon to cheer you up."

In Timmy's kitchen there were some apples in a cardboard box. They took the box and emptied the apples outside the back door. On Oliver's bed they found a green blanket, so they could make a beautiful dragon for Timmy's little sister. She *was* pleased. She could poke her little finger in its eye. She led it down the road.

First she walked with it and then she ran with it. Then she fell over her own feet and banged her knee.

"Oh bother!" said Tom. "Now she's started to cry again."

A lady was coming down the road with a shopping basket and she bent down and picked her up. "Poor old wounded soldier!" she said, dusting down her dress. She looked very kind but

Timmy's little sister opened her mouth as wide as it would go and shrieked. She didn't like being picked up by somebody she didn't know.

"Oh dear, the poor little darling!" said the lady anxiously. "*Now* what shall we do?—I know. You shall have something I was just taking down to the jumble-sale." She put her hand in her basket. "I found it in my garden," she said. "I think the cat must have brought it in."

Timmy's little sister stopped crying and smiled through her tears. She had got her dear old Bobo Angela back again!

The Indian Camp

Timmy's little sister ran home to play with Bobo Angela in the garden. She wanted to put her to bed in a seed-box.

The little boys went into the
field where the postman's goat
lived and played with the dragon.
"Parp-parp!" went the dragon.

"Parp-parp!" It sounded very
fierce. It jumped. It stood on its
back legs. It waved its paw and
scratched its nose. It was really
very clever.

When Timmy's little sister had tucked Bobo Angela up in bed with a dish-cloth and sung her a little song to make her go to sleep she went indoors and caught hold of her mother's skirt. "Ook!" she said, pointing her finger, "Ook!"

Timmy's mother was busy ironing. "Oh dear, it's you, is it," she said. "What's the matter now?"

Timmy's little sister pulled her until she came outside. "Ook!" she said proudly. The postman's goat was standing in the garden. Crunch, crunch, he was just finishing off the last of Timmy's mother's apples, cores and all.

Timmy's mother was cross. "However did that silly old goat get in and how did my apples get out?" she cried. "I put them all most carefully in a cardboard box in the kitchen only this

morning. It's those naughty little funny ones," she said to Timmy's little sister, "I know it is," and she caught hold of the goat in one hand and the baby in the other and ran to the fence to look for them. She looked all round. "Now, I wonder where they went," she said.

They went down to the lion-trap but there was nobody there except a squirrel who was using it to store his nuts in. Timmy's little

sister picked up an acorn and put
that in too.

With a flick of his tail the
squirrel ran up the tree. "He'll
come back as soon as we've
gone," said Timmy's mother.

They went to the duck-pond but there was nobody there except the ducks. Some of the little ducks were standing on their heads. Timmy's little sister could do that too.

"They're looking for their dinners," said Timmy's mother. "But I wonder *where* those naughty little funny ones have gone!"

Suddenly she clapped her hands over her ears. *What* a noise Oliver, Timmy, Tom and the sausage-dog were making! But Timmy's little sister liked a noise. She stamped her feet on the ground. "Baba!" she shouted, "Baba!"

"Parp-parp! Yowl-yowl! Wa-wa-wa-wa! Bang-bang!" Timmy's mother could hardly hear herself think. She ran across

the road to the field where the
goat lived.

The three little funny ones had
taken the dragon to pieces and
made an Indian camp instead.
They had made the box into a
tom-tom and the blanket into a
wig-wam, and they had found
three feathers. Round and round

danced the sausage-dog, Oliver,
Timmy and Tom. They were
enjoying themselves.

"Did *you* leave the gate open?" asked Timmy's mother, "and let the goat out? And did you take my apples out of my box and leave them in the garden for the goat to eat?"

The little boys hung their heads.

"You really are too naughty. Come along home with me and I'll give you something useful to do for a change."

The little boys' faces fell. It was getting dark already and they had so wanted to go on playing Indians. Even the sausage-dog looked sad. It *was* disappointing. Timmy's mother began to feel quite sorry for them.

"Well, never mind," she said, "you can leave it all up and come back and play in it later on."

That made them smile again.
Timmy's mother put the goat
into his field and shut the gate.
Then she gave them some
potatoes to peel while she went
upstairs and bathed Timmy's
little sister. Peeling the potatoes

was rather fun. Oliver chose the
round ones and made them all
into little faces. Timmy chose the
long ones and made them into
little rabbits. But Tom took any
potato that came and made it
into what it looked like most.

By the time she had bathed the baby Timmy's mother had forgotten all about the goat eating her apples.

"What lovely potatoes!" she cried when she came out again. "We must take them to your Indian camp and roast them in a camp-fire."

So all the little funny ones ran
about gathering sticks and their
mothers came out and lit a camp-
fire and then they sat round it

and sang songs while the
potatoes cooked. Timmy's little
sister came out all pink and clean

from her bath and got covered in
smuts.

She sang the loudest of all.
She *did* enjoy the roast
potatoes.

She ate a little face,

a little rabbit,

and a dear little baby
in a basket.

THE END